The Donkey Egg

By Janet Stevens and Susan Stevens Crummel Illustrated by Janet Stevens

HOUGHTON MIFFLIN HARCOURT
Boston   New York

For Mom and Dad, who always kept us warm, safe, and happy.

hmhco.com

The illustrations in this book were done in mixed media.
The text type was set in Humper.

Library of Congress Cataloging-in-Publication Data
Names: Stevens, Janet, author, illustrator. | Crummel, Susan Stevens, author.
Title: The donkey egg / by Janet Stevens and Susan Stevens Crummel ;
illustrated by Janet Stevens. Description: Boston : Houghton Mifflin Harcourt,
[2018] | Summary: After fast-talking Fox leaves him with a large, green egg,
Bear spends minutes, hours, days, and weeks lovingly caring for it with the
help of his neighbor Hare. Identifiers: LCCN 2017061482 |
ISBN 9780547327679 (hardback) Subjects: | CYAC: Bears—Fiction. |
Hares—Fiction. | Perseverance (Ethics)—Fiction. | Humorous stories. |
BISAC: JUVENILE FICTION / Animals / Bears. | JUVENILE FICTION /
Concepts / Date & Time. | JUVENILE FICTION /
Humorous Stories. Classification: LCC PZ7.S84453 Do 2018 |
DDC [E]—dc23LC record available at
https://lccn.loc.gov/2017061482

Manufactured in China
SCP 10 9 8 7 6 5 4 3
4500789330

Starring

Bear
Old. Lazy. Cranky. Worked hard once, but not anymore. Needs motivation.

Hare
Friendly. Speedy. Always running. Wants a rematch with Tortoise.

Blanket
Warm. Dramatic. Hides things. Multi-talented. Has a checkered past.

Fox
Clever. Loves to play tricks. Looking for mischief and some quick cash.

And a cameo appearance by **Donkey**. Where did he come from?

Egg
Green. Mysterious. What's inside?

UP ON THE HILL lived a grumpy old Bear.
His farm was a wreck and it needed repair.
But Bear didn't care. He just slept in his chair
and growled at his neighbors, Fox and Hare.

"Wake up, Bear!" cried Fox. "I KNOW you want to turn this place back into a mighty fine farm, grow some mighty fine crops, and have a mighty fine life.
But YOU need help and I'VE got just the thing!"
"**Gr-r-r-r-r-r**," growled Bear. "What thing?"

"That's not a donkey!" cried Bear.

"Not YET—but it WILL be," said Fox. "It's a donkey egg! A genuine, certified donkey egg! Still green—has to ripen and hatch. That's where you come in. Keep it warm, safe, and happy, like a little mama bird on her nest.

It will take time—minutes, hours, days, weeks, months—so be patient.

Then VOILÀ!

A DONKEY!"

"As you know, Bear, lots of animals come from eggs—

Chickens.

Dinosaurs.

Platypuses.

Alligators.

=

And DONKEYS! It's the truth!"

"I can see it now.
Your fields are plowed.
Your house is painted.
You and your donkey, sitting on
the porch, watching the sunset.
What a deal! And it's a steal—
today only—$19.95!"
"No way!" said Bear.
Fox sighed. "OK, I'll settle for
that twenty dollar bill. SOLD!
It's a done deal!"

*Fox scooped up the cash,
disappeared in a flash.
And all that was left was Bear,
in his chair . . .*

and a gigantic, green donkey egg.

"That fast-talking Fox," muttered Bear.
"NOW what am I supposed to do?"
Then he remembered.
"Keep it warm."
So, like a big mama bird,
Bear carefully sat.
This way and that.
He sat and he sat.

Tickety-tock.
Clickety-clock.
Minutes passed.
No donkey.

Did You Know?

1 minute = 60 seconds

It takes about a second to sneeze.
AHHHH-CHOO-OO-OO!

A hummingbird's wings beat about 70 times in one second—
so fast you can hardly see them moving!

It takes about a minute for an ice cream cone
to melt on a hot day.

It takes about two minutes to brush your teeth!

Neighbor Hare had just begun his daily run when he
SCRE-E-E-E-E-CHED to a halt.

"Bear, you're *out of* your chair!"

"I'm sitting on my donkey egg," growled Bear.

"What? Donkeys don't come from EGGS!"

"Yes, they DO!" cried Bear. "Like dinosaurs,
chickens, alligators, platypuses—even tortoises.
I'm keeping it warm—so it will hatch.
Been sitting for a whole hour—no donkey."

"Well, you keep sitting
and I'll keep running," said Hare.
"Got another race with Tortoise!"

Off went Hare, leaving Bear to sit.

And sit and sit. Mustn't quit.

Tickety-tock.
Clickety-clock.
Hours passed.
No donkey.

Did You Know?

1 hour = 60 minutes = 3,600 seconds

It takes a spider about an hour to spin a fancy web.

You blink your eye over 1,000 times in an hour!

Your heart beats over 5,000 times in an hour!

"What do I do now?" Then Bear remembered,
"Keep it safe."
Bear cradled the egg and sang,
"Rock-a-bye, Donkey, my little one.
Ripen and hatch, there's work to be done.
If there is danger, I will be there!
You'll be my Donkey, I'll be your Bear."

Again, Hare SCRE-E-E-E-E-E-CHED to a halt.
"Bear, you're *rocking and singing* in your chair!"

"I'm keeping my donkey egg safe," replied Bear.

"Been rocking all day—no donkey."

"Well, you keep rocking and I'll keep running," said Hare.

"Gotta win that race!"

Off went Hare, leaving Bear to rock.

And rock and rock.

Rockity-rock.
Tickety-tock.
Clickety-clock.
Days passed.
No donkey.

Did You Know?

1 day = 24 hours = 1,440 minutes = 86,400 seconds

One day is about how long it takes the
Earth to spin all the way around on its axis.

Most chickens lay one egg per day.

Bamboo can grow up to almost 3 feet a day.
If you grew 3 feet a day, in just one week you
would be taller than a house!

Kids laugh about 300 times in one day.
Grownups only laugh 17 times!

"Now what?"
Then Bear remembered,
"Keep it happy."

He told Egg a tale of a girl and three bears.
Fables with tortoises, foxes, and hares.

Bear acted out plays
where he played every part.

Again and again, till he knew them by heart.

Bear pointed his toes as he leaped through the air.

He played peek-a-boo,
hiding under his chair.

For the third time, Hare SCRE-E-E-E-E-E-CHED
to a halt.
"Bear, you're *under* your chair!"
"I'm playing with my donkey egg," said Bear.
"Keeping it happy—so it will hatch! Been playing all
week—STILL no donkey."

"But there will be!" Bear grinned.
"So you keep running and I'll keep playing.
I'm gonna hatch that egg and you're gonna
beat that Tortoise!"

Off went Hare, leaving Bear to play.
And play and play. Night and day.

Tickety-tock.
Clickety-clock.
Weeks passed.
No donkey.

Did You Know?

1 week = 7 days = 168 hours = 10,080 minutes = 604,800 seconds

A mama hummingbird takes about a week to build her tiny nest,
which is the size of a Ping-Pong ball.

A mama eagle takes over two weeks to build her giant
nest, which is 8 feet wide—Dad helps!

It takes about a week for a snake to shed its entire skin. Humans
gradually shed their skin—about 7 million skin cells in a week.

Through wind and rain and snow Bear stayed.

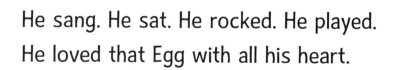

He sang. He sat. He rocked. He played.
He loved that Egg with all his heart.

Never was there quite a pair.
Bear and Egg. Egg and Bear.

Only napping here and there,
Bear grew tired.

Really tired.
REALLY, REALLY tired.

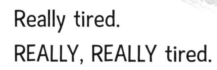

He couldn't keep from
falling . . . falling . . .

Fast asleep.

Z-Z-Z-Z-Z-Z

PLOP!

R-R-R-O-O-O-L-L-L-L

"Oh NO!" shouted Bear.

"H-E-E-E-E-L-L-L-P! Egg on the loose!"

Hare's ears perked up.

"Egg on the LOOSE? Hare to the rescue!"

And the chase was on.

It was Egg out in front, Bear close behind,
and Hare bringing up the rear.

Around the turn. Egg leading. Hare speeding.
Bear stampeding.

Across the road. Egg tumbling. Hare stumbling. Bear fumbling.

Through the field. Bear thrashing. Hare dashing. Egg crashing . . .

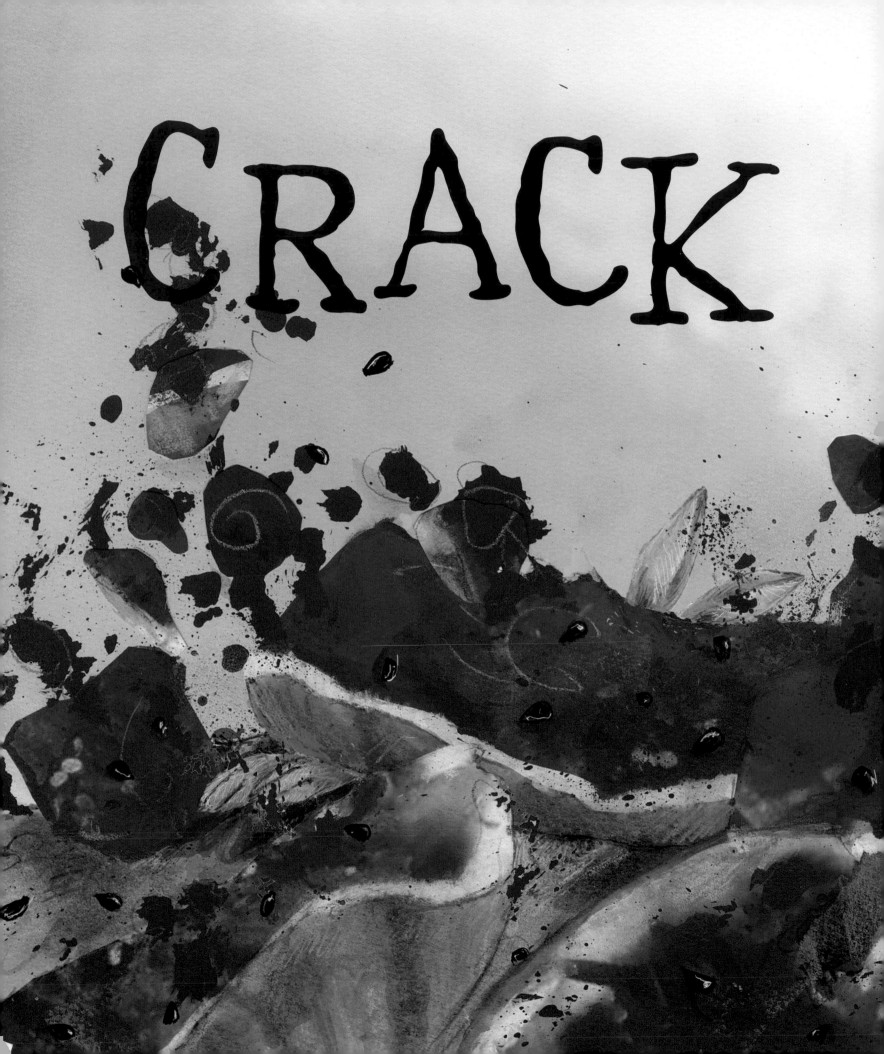

CRACK

"My donkey hatched!" cried Bear. "I've got 'im by the ears!"
"Ouch! Those are MY ears," hollered Hare. "Can't you see?
It's not a donkey egg. It's a *watermelon!*"
"But it can't be! Fox said it was a genuine, certified donkey egg."
"Fox?" gasped Hare. "You believed Fox?"

Bear hung his head.
"He tricked me.
Fox tricked me.
No donkey egg.
No baby donkey.
No nothing."
There wasn't a sound as Bear
looked around.
And there, on the ground,
guess what he found?

"Seeds!" Bear had an idea. "I've got work to do."
"Well, you start working and I'll . . ." Hare paused.
"Oh, who cares about a silly old race?"

For hours, then days,
Bear and Hare tilled the land.
They weeded and planted
and watered by hand.

For weeks, then months, the plants grew and grew.
May . . . June . . . July . . . they were growing into . . .

Did You Know?

1 month = 31 days (or 30 days or 29 days or 28 days)

12 months = 365 days = 1 year

It takes a whole YEAR for the earth to travel around the sun!

Your hair grows about 1/2 inch per month,
which means 6 inches per year.

A mama donkey carries a baby donkey in her body for about
a year before it is born. (Of course you already know donkeys
don't actually come from eggs!)

Watermelons! Everywhere!
To market, to market went Bear and Hare to sell those melons—
AND WHAT DID THEY BUY?

HEE-HAW!
HEE-HAW!

Off ran Bear, with Donkey and Hare,
to fix up his farm that needed repair.
And all that was left was . . .